When a little kitten named Candy strikes up a very big friendship with a hippo named Veronica, it is just the start of
hippopotomus-sized problems for Farmer Applegreen and Farmer
Pumpkin. Now you might consider this friendship a strange
match indeed, but true friends pay little attention to the looks
of things. Strange, though, are the merry mix-ups between the
farm on the hill and the farm in the valley—on Mrs. Applegreen's birthday.

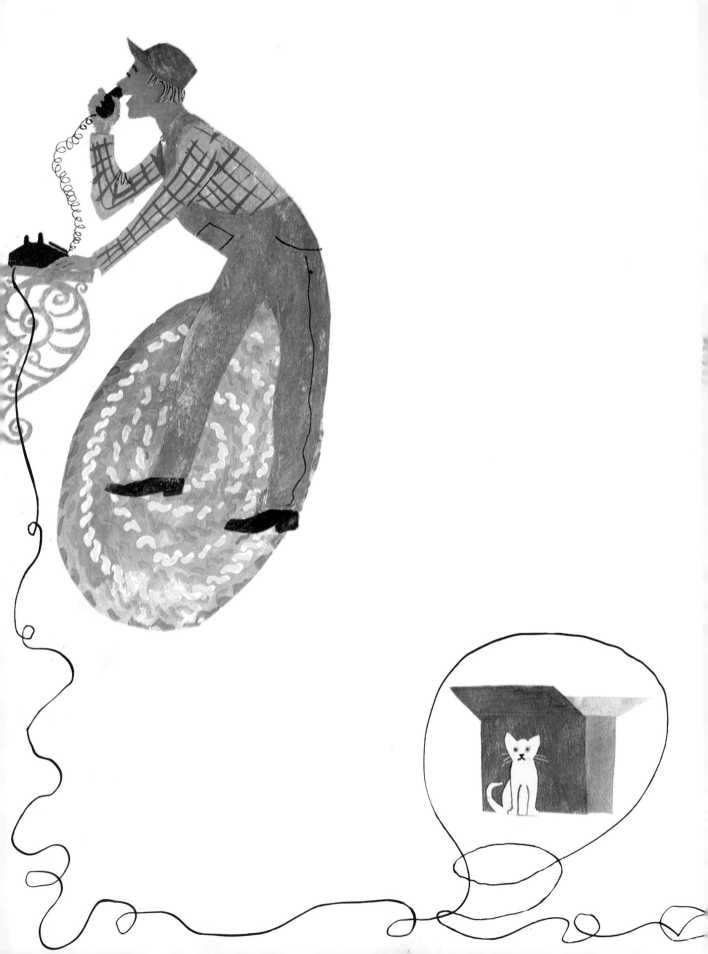

Veronica
and the
Birthday Present

by

Roger Duvoisin

ALFRED · A · KNOPF

NEW YORK

This is a Borzoi Book Published by Alfred A. Knopf, Inc.

Copyright © 1971 by Roger Duvoisin.
All rights reserved under International and Pan-American Copyright Conventions.
Published in the United States by Alfred A. Knopf, Inc., New York,
and simultaneously in Canada by Random House of Canada Limited, Toronto.
Distributed by Random House, Inc., New York. Trade Edition: ISBN: 0-394-82282-X.
Library Edition: ISBN: 0-394-92282-4. Library of Congress Catalog Card Number: 71-154547.

Manufactured in the United States of America. First Edition.

Farmer Applegreen was very happy that spring morning.
He was driving home in his truck with a birthday present for his
wife—a lovely kitten, white as sugar icing, with blue eyes.

"We will call her Candy," said Mr. Applegreen, and he patted
the brown box in which the kitten was sleeping.

Suddenly, a tire went *bing, zzzz, flap flap flap.* A flat tire.

"This *would* happen to me when I am in a hurry to get home,"
groaned Mr. Applegreen. He jumped out to change the tire.

When finally he entered his farm kitchen, Mr. Applegreen gave the brown box to his wife, saying,

"Happy birthday, dear." And he kissed her.

Mrs. Applegreen opened the box with joy, but . . . the box was empty. Nothing in it. Nothing.

"NOTHING?" exclaimed Mr. Applegreen. "Why, the loveliest kitten you ever saw was in that box. She must have escaped when I changed my tire."

Mr. Applegreen telephoned the postmaster and asked him to tack a notice on the post office wall about the lost kitten.

"Surely someone will bring her back," he said.

Indeed, Candy had escaped from the box and fled through the grasses and wild flowers which bordered the road. She ran up a hill and down into a little valley, where she saw Mr. Pumpkin's farm. By this time she was very tired.

So tired that she bumped into a big, fat, grey rock which lay in the grass. Candy looked around it for a place to rest, and suddenly she heard the rock say,

"Good morning, little kitten. Where did you come from?"

"Are you a talking rock?" asked Candy, startled.

"No, I am Veronica, Mr. Pumpkin's hippopotamus. I live on his farm with Petunia the goose, the gander, the donkey, the horse, the goat, the cat, the dog, with pigs, turkeys, chickens, and cows. They are my friends. Will you be my friend too?"

In response, Candy snuggled close to Veronica and fell asleep.
This is how Candy and Veronica became good friends.

When Mr. Pumpkin made the rounds of his farm that evening,
he saw Candy still asleep against Veronica.
"Popcorn and melons, Veronica! Where did you find this pretty
kitten?" he asked. And he took Candy to his wife.

Mrs. Pumpkin petted her and fed her. She prepared a soft bed for her in the kitchen. What a friendly kitchen!

But Candy's love was for Veronica. And so, after her meal, she walked out through the open kitchen door to search for her friend Veronica.

The hippopotamus was in her shed for the night when Candy found her.

"I am so glad you came back," Veronica said. "I missed you. You may sleep next to me. Good night."

Candy spent three happy days on Mr. Pumpkin's farm.

Three days? Why only three days?

Because on the third day Mr. Pumpkin saw Mr. Applegreen's notice in the post office.

He telephoned Mr. Applegreen at once.

"Hello, Mr. Applegreen? This is Mr. Pumpkin. Good morning. I think I found your kitten. Come and see."

Mr. Applegreen knew it was Candy as soon as he saw her.
"White as sugar icing, with blue eyes, that's Candy."
He put Candy in the brown box. This time he tied it with a
string. He placed the box in the back of his truck.

Now while Mr. and Mrs. Pumpkin and Mr. Applegreen shared
some coffee in the kitchen, Veronica said to herself,

"I'll not let my kitten friend go away without me."

And she climbed down into Mr. Applegreen's truck from the
bank against which it was parked.

That is why, after Mr. Applegreen arrived home, he and his wife had such a fit when they went to fetch the brown box.

"A HIPPOPOTAMUS!" screamed Mrs. Applegreen in fright.

"A HIPPOPOTAMUS!" shouted Mr. Applegreen, and he ran to telephone Mr. Pumpkin.

"A hippopotamus in your truck?" answered Mr. Pumpkin. "Cabbages and beans! It can only be *my* Veronica. Wait until I come."

So, Mr. Pumpkin drove to Mr. Applegreen's farm to lead
Veronica out of Mr. Applegreen's truck into his own.

But while he was doing this, Candy, who was still in the
brown box, was saying to herself,

"I will not stay here without my friend Veronica. No and no."

She scratched, and pushed, and bit so furiously that she got
out of the box and and slipped from one truck to the other right
beside Veronica. UNSEEN. And that is how Candy went back with
Veronica to Mr. Pumpkin's farm.

"Turnips and peas!" said Mr. Pumpkin when he saw the kitten
jump out of the truck. "I had better telephone Mr. Applegreen."

"Hello, Mr. Applegreen? Ah . . . you were going to telephone?
Oh, yes indeed, Candy's here. So sorry Mrs. Applegreen got
only an empty box again. But wait, I'll bring the kitten back."

And now, Veronica and Candy lived far away from each other.
The very next afternoon, Veronica said to Petunia the goose,
"I'll go and fetch my friend by myself if I have to."
"I'll come with you," answered Petunia. "I know the way."
"I think I'll go too" said Goat. "I love that kitten."

So across fields and through woods, Veronica, Petunia and Goat
walked to Mr. Applegreen's farm.

When they arrived, Mr. and Mrs. Applegreen were already
in bed, but Candy was meowing in the kitchen.

"Candy," called Veronica through the kitchen door, "I have
come to fetch you."

"So have I," said Petunia and Goat.

Soon, Alexander and Andromeda, Mr. Applegreen's
pet dog and goat, came to say "how do you do." And they all had
the most pleasant talk about how to get Candy out of the kitchen.

"I wonder what that awful noise is," said Mrs. Applegreen, waking her husband. Both went downstairs to have a look.

While Mr. Applegreen grabbed up Candy into his arms, Mrs. Applegreen opened the kitchen door. When she saw Veronica's big nose sticking through the door, she cried,

"OOOHH . . . THAT HORRID BEAST AGAIN!" And she pushed Veronica's nose out with all her strength and closed the door.

"WAIT TILL I TELEPHONE MR. PUMPKIN!" shouted her husband.

"HELLO, MR. PUMPKIN? This is Applegreen. Say, who brought back that hippopotamus? With that goose and that goat?"

"Spinach and pepper!" cried Mr. Pumpkin. "I wonder. Wait until I get dressed and drive over."

Again, Mr. Pumpkin went to Mr. Applegreen's, and the two drove Veronica, Petunia and Goat into the truck.

In the meantime, Candy was saying to herself,

"I am *not* going to live in this kitchen without my Veronica."

Finding that the door had not been closed all the way, she ran out and hid under the seat of Mr. Pumpkin's truck.

When Mr. Pumpkin got home he was so tired that he left his animals in his truck and went to bed right away.

The next morning before breakfast he saw Candy waiting for Veronica to come out of the truck."

"Carrots and beets!" exclaimed Mr. Pumpkin, "I had better telephone Mr. Applegreen." But his telephone rang first.

"Hello, Mr. Pumpkin? It's Mr. Applegreen. Say, where is Candy?"

"Here," said Mr. Pumpkin. "And don't ask me how."

"Wait," said Mr. Applegreen. "I'll go and fetch her. My wife hasn't seen much of her yet." And he came right over. Poor Veronica and Candy—they lost each other again.

But it was not for long.

The very next afternoon, Veronica said to Petunia,

"I'll go fetch Candy a hundred times if I have to.

I'LL NOT BE WITHOUT MY FRIEND. I AM GOING NOW."

"You are right," said Petunia. "I am going too."

"So am I," said Goat. "It's fun."

"I think I am going too," said—

Charles the Gander,

Clover the cow,

Rose the sheep,

Donkey,

mother and father pig

and piglet.

And across fields and through woods, they followed Veronica.

When they arrived, the farm was dark. Mr. and Mrs. Applegreen had gone to the movies. But Candy was meowing in the kitchen.

Veronica was now so impatient to see her friend, that she broke through the door and frame to get in. Candy ran over to purr around her friend's legs.

Petunia, Goat, Charles, Clover, Rose, Donkey, father and mother pig and piglet went in too. Very soon some of Mr. Applegreen's animals joined them—

Alexander the dog,	Anabella and Elizabeth the cows,
Ulysses the pig,	Theodore the calf,
Andromeda the goat,	and Nathaniel the ram.

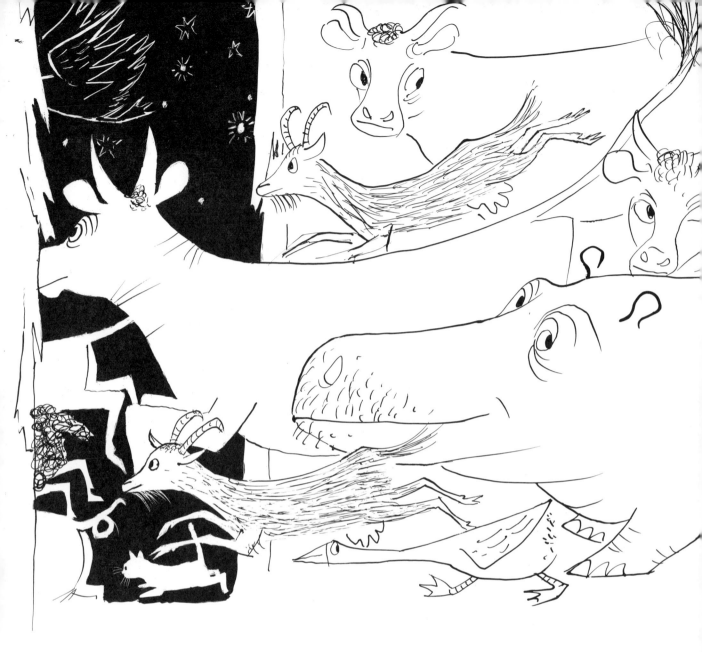

They all settled down on the warm kitchen floor or on the doorstep.

After the movie Mr. and Mrs. Applegreen came in too.

"OOOHHH HORROR, HORROR!" screamed Mrs. Applegreen, and she put her head into her hands. Then, she picked up the broom and chased the animals back into the night.

But she forgot to pick up Candy who went too.

"WAIT TIL I TELEPHONE MR. PUMPKIN!" shouted Mr. Applegreen.

"HELLO, HELLO! MR. PUMPKIN? Your hippopotamus broke into
my kitchen, and so did your goose and goat and cow and
gander and sheep and donkey and pigs. Broke down
the door—frame and all!"

"Garlic and onions!" said Mr. Pumpkin. "Who took
them there? Wait until I come and fetch them."

"Don't come," said Mr. Applegreen. "They are all gone now.
Maybe they are on their way back to your farm."

And they were. So were Mr. Applegreen's animals—
Alexander,   Anabella,   Elizabeth,   Theodora.
Nathaniel,   Ulysses,   Andromeda,
    They had said, "Veronica is such fun. Let's go with her."
    Early the next morning when Mr. Pumpkin was shaving,
he saw Veronica and all her friends enter his farmyard.
He almost fell backwards into his bathtub.

"Lettuce and corn!" he exclaimed, "wait until I telephone Mr. Applegreen!

"Hello, Mr. Applegreen? This is Pumpkin. Listen, lots of animals have just come in, *with Candy*. Some are mine and some are not. Must be yours, I think. I'll bring them back."

"This is *Mrs*. Applegreen speaking," said Mrs. Applegreen. "Mr. Applegreen got a headache this morning when he saw that his animals were gone. Don't come. *I* will drive over

to fetch Candy. Just Candy. Then you will see what will happen."

What happened? When Veronica saw that Candy was lost
to her once more, she said to Petunia,

"I said I would go and fetch my friend a hundred times
if I had to. I am leaving. And I'll hide Candy so well that
THEY will never find her and take her away from me."

"I'll go with you," said Petunia.

"So will I," said all the Pumpkin animals—Goat,
Charles the gander, Clover and Canary the cows, Rose the sheep,
Donkey, Straw the horse, Noisy the dog, mother and father pigs

and piglet, Ida the hen and King the rooster, Bill and
Sue the turkeys, Cotton the cat. "Three cheers for Veronica and
Candy!" they cried.

"I will go too," said Mr. Applegreen's animals—Alexander,
Anabella, Elizabeth, Theodora, Nathaniel, and Ulysses.

"What a fine time we are having!"

And across fields and through woods, they traveled back to Mr.
Applegreen's farm. When they arrived, they walked around
the farmhouse, calling,

"Candy, we have come to fetch you, Candy, oh, Candy . . . "

But Mr. and Mrs. Applegreen had been waiting for them.
They drove Alexander, Anabella, Elizabeth, Theodora, Andromeda,
Nathaniel and Ulysses into the barn and locked the door.

Then, Mrs. Applegreen put Candy on Veronica's back and said,
"Veronica, you and Candy love each other so much that
I think you should stay together and be happy. So, Veronica,
I give you *my* birthday present."

And Veronica and Candy, and all the other Pumpkin
animals gaily returned to Mr. Pumpkin's farm.

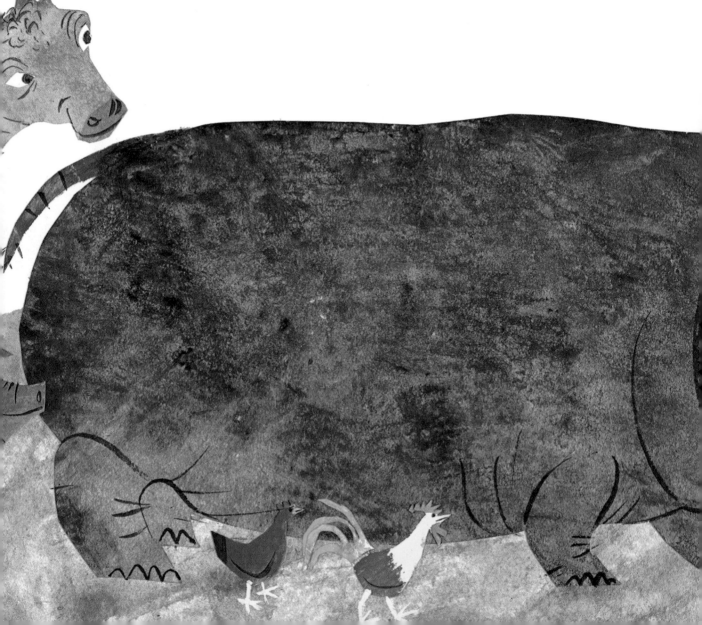

The next day, Mr. and Mrs. Pumpkin went to the pet shop
where Mr. Applegreen had found Candy. They came out
with a brown box tied with a pink ribbon which they took at once
to Mrs. Applegreen.

"This is *our* happy birthday present to you, Mrs. Applegreen."

Mrs. Applegreen opened the box with joy and . . . she saw a
lovely kitten, white as sugar icing, with blue eyes.

It was Candy's twin brother.

"We will call him Periwinkle, because of his blue eyes,"
said Mr. Applegreen.

And there was peace, love and happiness ever after, on the
Pumpkin and Applegreen farms.